I0621311

She's Getting It Again!

She's Just Bad, Volume 2

Lucy Lafferty

Published by Lynda French, 2025.

This is a work of fiction. Similarities to real people, places, or events are entirely coincidental.

SHE'S GETTING IT AGAIN!

First edition. November 5, 2025.

Copyright © 2025 Lucy Lafferty.

ISBN: 978-1998074570

Written by Lucy Lafferty.

Table of Contents

To those who don't learn their lesson the first time... now you're getting it again!

About This Book

Description:

*Another book of short stories in the **She's Just Bad** series.*

More naughtiness leads to lots more punishment, but bad girls never seem to learn. No matter how blisteringly hot that bare bottom gets spanked.

These ten stories range from spanking as mentoring, being taught a harsh lesson, showing contrition, and discovering that actions can have unexpected consequences.

Enjoy reading how proper discipline turns a defiant little miss into a sore and sorry girl. *Until the next time the naughty minx misbehaves!*

Content Warning:

Please do not read if stories about spanking will trigger bad memories or trauma.

The Wayward Ward

Bethany is winning the argument in the imaginary conversation she's having with herself. She's assertive and certain of her irrefutable facts while demonstrating mature and thoughtful consideration of Andrew's counterpoints. He thrusts, she parries, until she wears him out with her logic and wins.

Except what do I want to win? she wonders. *I know I say I want my freedom but to do what, exactly? My homeschooling has finished and I wasn't clever enough to go to university. I can't think of anything I want to do for a job, and I don't have any skills anyhow. I think I'd be interested in traveling but I can't very well go by myself. If only Andrew didn't think of me as just a silly, little girl. Oh, I wish I was bold and forthright and wayward!*

Her face frowns in a pout and watching her from the upstairs window Andrew smirks. Especially when she leans against the decorative railing before quickly pulling back with a yelp. He chuckles thinking how sore her little bottom is and how it's going to get worse before it gets better.

His little ward has grown up and is ready to spread her wings. *Well that's certainly not going to happen,* he chuckles to himself. *Bethany is mine. I have nurtured that girl since her infancy, biding my time until she became ready to claim.*

Andrew Underwood is Bethany Chalmers guardian, as designated by her parents in their Last Will & Testament. He is also her betrothed, which she will discover when she attains her majority in two weeks and learns the stipulation of her inheritance. But for his plans to succeed first he needs to get her under his complete control.

Andrew kept a close eye on Bethany's development but was careful to ensure they never met. He didn't want her to think of him as a father figure, or an avuncular family friend. He also didn't want to know her as a child, not when he was planning to marry her some day.

3

They'd become engaged, privately of course, at her birth. Ten years ago, when her parents were tragically killed in a hotel fire, she became his ward.

Over the years Andrew made sure Bethany's tutors steered her away from any lessons where she showed notable skill or talent. He wants a malleable wife, not an accomplished one. No one could take away her natural singing voice, strong with a wide vocal range, but he doesn't mind that. Andrew looks forward to eliciting loud cries of passion and pleading.

Bethany's godmother, Ariadne Chalmers, knew of both arrangements her cousin had made with Andrew Underwood. So although the woman wished the young girl could have enjoyed a carefree life with plenty of parties and beaux she knew that was never going to happen. Bethany's future was all mapped out while she was still an infant.

Bethany came out at the city's Debutantes' Ball just three weeks before her eighteenth birthday, and Andrew took charge of her from that moment forward. Ariadne couldn't complain, he was a handsome, wealthy, eligible man but at thirty-two he was also almost twice the girl's age.

I suppose that's not necessarily a bad thing... she mused at the time, *but he's so domineering and commanding. I worry he'll crush her spirit although in truth she's hasn't really shown much. She's quite a docile, obedient girl and very pretty in her face and figure. Oh well, I've done my duty by bringing the girl out so she's in Andrew's hands now.*

Bethany was in Andrew's hands last night and she's still suffering the effects. It all began quite innocently when they were discussing her clothing allowance. Andrew decided that since he was paying for everything he should be allowed to see what he'd bought.

"But you have, I mean sure there are some gowns I haven't had an opportunity to wear yet, but other than that I've pretty much just bought what I need for everyday."

"Yes, but according to the print-out from the store I've bought a large amount of expensive lingerie and I definitely haven't seen any of that."

Bethany feels her mouth fall into an O shape of surprise, and blushes because she knows she did go overboard with all the lacy bits she got. *But everything is so pretty I simply can't choose,* she recalls thinking at the time.

"Well, I guess I can go fetch the stuff from my room and show you—" she begins.

Andrew interrupts telling her: "I've already seen photos from the invoices. I want to see the merchandise modeled."

He's serious! she thinks, scandalized by the thought. "Andrew I'm not stripping down to my undies and that's final!" Bethany forcefully declares.

Andrew purses his lips while studying her. He waits so long she starts to fidget, giving in to her unfortunate habit of snapping the hem of her panties through her dress. Her hand is rather high up and Andrew realizes she's wearing one of those silky thongs he's paid for. The strap will be sitting high on her hip leaving her backside exposed and he enjoys the picture that's formed in his mind.

"I don't care for your tone, Bethany. You do not give me ultimatums. I tell you what to do and you do it, understand?"

"Um, no Andrew, I don't understand. You're being high-handed and piggish and just plain mean bullying me like this." Folding her arms tight across her chest Bethany is the picture of defiance.

Quick as a flash Andrew strides across the room and before she knows what's going on Bethany finds herself face down across her guardian's knee. Andrew ignores her demand of *what do you think you're doing?* and starts swatting her behind while she indignantly kicks and fights against him.

"Behave yourself, you spoilt little girl," he hisses angrily "or I'll... to hell with it, I'll do it anyhow." And with that remark he lifts the hem of her dress up to her waist and is greeted by the delectable sight of

Bethany's creamy fleshy bottom, bare except for the thin strap of fabric that constitutes her pricey thong.

After pausing a long moment to ogle the pretty view Andrew begins a rat-a-tat spanking striking sharply and steadily. He berates Bethany *firstly for choosing such outrageous underwear, secondly for actually wearing it, and finally for wearing it under a dress.*

The smacks rain down harder with each criticism and though the girl would love to refute his claims she's too busy gasping at each stinging blow and can't catch her breath.

"Scandalous slut playing the tease!" he chastises her with his words and the palm of his hand.

She's sure the staff can hear the loud smacking sound of every stroke and is humiliated that they know she's being spanked like a naughty child. Andrew completely ignores her cries of *stop!* and *don't!*

The rosy red of her derriere satisfies Andrew that Bethany's sassy backtalk has been suitably disciplined. His scheme to dominate and control every thought and every action of his future bride is off to a great start. She's learning that there will always be consequences.

Hoisting her back on her feet again he sends her to bed. It's early, but with a housemaid and a footman lingering to gossip in the foyer Bethany is only too happy to escape to her room. In the privacy of her boudoir she commiserates with herself over how hot her flesh is as she rubs her sore bottom for relief.

Now it's the following morning and she's determined to speak seriously with Andrew. It's important that he understands he must treat her like the grown-up woman she is.

Bethany is well aware that suitors will appear when she comes into her inheritance on her eighteenth birthday so the sooner Andrew recognizes that she's an adult - and a lady - the better.

She finishes marshaling her thoughts just as the breakfast gong sounds. Chin up she marches past the tittering serving staff and takes her seat at the table. Andrew is already sitting down and he quirks an eyebrow when he notices how she flinches when she lands on her chair.

Bethany pretends she doesn't see and instead requests an interview with him in his study after the meal. The wolfishness of his smile gives her pause but he agrees readily enough so she tamps down any misgivings.

Half-an-hour later the two of them are in the study. Andrew is seated in the big chair behind his desk while Bethany wanders around feigning interest in the bookshelves until he loudly clears his throat to get her attention.

Bethany comes up to his desk and leaning forward states: "Andrew, I'm coming into my inheritance soon which means I'll be dating with a view to getting married so you need to—"

"No," he interrupts.

She blinks in wide-eyed surprise at the abruptness of his tone.

"No, Bethany," he repeats, "You will not be dating because you already have a fiancé."

"No I don't... who?"

"Me," he answers getting up to walk around to her side. Tilting her head back to meet his eyes Bethany's surprised look encounters Andrew's intense gaze.

"You are marrying me. It's all spelled out in the documentation accompanying your inheritance. This was decided by your parents and mine from the moment you were born. It wasn't my choice, I was a minor at only fourteen, but now that you've come-of-age I'm..." he pauses to rake his eyes over her from head to toe before continuing: "satisfied with the arrangement."

Rage like she's never experienced before erupts within Bethany's breast and explodes in a furious diatribe against Andrew and whatever nonsense their parents have concocted. She practically spits the words at him finishing up by insisting *I won't marry you and you can't make me, it's the 21st century for godsake!*

But poor Bethany learns that Andrew can, indeed, coerce her co-operation.

He expected this reaction, although not quite as vehemently as she's shown, and wastes no time pushing her across the desk. Bent over like this her feet don't touch the ground and she can't propel herself up and off. Same as yesterday evening Andrew pulls at her clothes until he bares her bottom.

"I enjoy taking my time with a leisurely over-the-knee spanking Bethany and you'll get plenty of those as my wife, but this is something different. This is me teaching you a lesson in obedience and you are going to learn it the hard way."

Andrew picks up a wooden ruler off the desk and begins pattering it all over Bethany's still-pink rear. "I know this doesn't feel like much compared to my palm but believe me enough of these steady strokes will soon heat up your tender flesh."

Only minutes later he's proven correct as Bethany can't stop squirming in a futile attempt to escape the flurry of thwacks. Each swat feels thuddier than the last and the tapping sound is steady and rhythmic. Bethany's muscles clench and she feels her bum jump and jiggle, but she can't avoid the constant punishment.

By time Andrew is finished he's breathing heavily from exertion and arousal. Bethany is sobbing because her red bottom burns and throbs. He sends her back upstairs to her room with that threat that if her attitude is no better by lunchtime she'll get a taste of his belt. The girl wails loudly as she flees.

Flopping back down in his executive chair Andrew gives a complacent sigh. He's going to enjoy being married to Bethany. It's so easy to pull her strings until she talks herself into a trip over his knee for a needful correction.

Although his own future has always been as strictly plotted as hers at least he's the one in charge, the head of the household, and he's going to savor every spank he administers and every tear he extracts.

Bethany is a lush little virgin just ripe to be molded and manipulated into the marriage he envisions.

She's awfully naive, he thinks. *It's obvious she hasn't realized that if I can see her underwear shopping history then I can also see what books she buys for her eReader.*

He smiles at the serendipity of discovering that his arranged bride has a predilection for stories with titles like *Disciplined by Her Tutor, Properly Punished by Him,* and the blatant *Bare-Bottomed Spankings.* Tales of Alpha males taming their wayward brats clearly indicate where her sexual interests lie.

It's kismet, he decides, *and yes she is definitely going to get a taste of my belt before the day is over.*

Lessons for the Trainee

Following in her older sister's footsteps Kelly enters the training program at the hospital with top marks and glowing recommendations from her school. The reality is she's turned out to be a frustrating disappointment.

Faced with dire situations fraught with life-or-death drama she performs professionally, but when it comes to the small duties performed dozens of times a day her mind wanders and she makes mistakes.

Bandages rolled backwards so the velcro doesn't work, caps left off tubes, sterilized items mixed with used cloths... silly, stupid errors that waste time and annoy everyone.

Finally the Head Nurse decides *serious measures are required* and demands that Dr. Crockett, the Ward Physician, *take Probationer Kelly in hand*. When he's told what's going on he eagerly agrees, thinking *what a shame it would be if such potential was ruined by carelessness.*

Burying the wicked delight he feels he soberly replies: "A serious situation indeed, Nurse. Bring Probationer Kelly to my Examining Room in..." he pauses to glance at his watch, "half-an-hour and with your help we'll begin."

Satisfied that something will be done Nurse replies: "Yes, Doctor."

Thirty minutes later Kelly is anxiously pleating the hem of her scrubs while listening to Dr. Crockett outline his training method that he's used successfully time and time again. Nurse nods in confirmation.

"I will teach you how to concentrate on your tasks, no matter how small, by the use of corporal punishment. You will have a session before and after each shift and this will train your brain.

As you work through your day a sore bottom will keep you mindful of your duties. Once you manage to get through your day without any errors we'll be able to skip the after-shift correction. That will give you a goal to strive for.

Nurse will assist me now in demonstrating my reinforcement technique. When I arrive tomorrow morning I will expect to see you here, on your own, ready to be prepped for the day by a sound spanking."

Confused, Kelly looks at her superior who indicates the girl should lie face-down on the examining table. Slowly she gets into position, lying prone, until Nurse drops down the end of the table leaving Kelly's legs hanging and her toes barely grazing the floor. Nurse places Kelly's hands at the top edge of the table and instructs her to *grip hard*. She remains in place looking down at her trainee.

Dr. Crockett opens his instrument drawer and removes an implement he calls *a three-tailed tawse*. Kelly's eyes widen with apprehension when he shows it to her. It's a long strap split into three strips and held together by a sturdy leather handle.

She opens her mouth to ask a question but the Doctor wastes no time discussing the discipline. He simply pulls down the pants of Kelly's scrubs dragging her panties along with them, causing her to gasp in protest at her nudity.

"Now I'm going to give you a taste of my own favorite medicine," he says, adding with a chuckle: "It's a cure that's guaranteed to work every time."

Wielding the strap efficiently and steadily he attacks her bared bottom with stroke after painful stroke until he's painted every inch of flesh deep pink. Each flail of the tawse falls just a split second after the others so it is sting added to sting added to sting.

The Doctor takes pride in his extracurricular work. He savors the crisp sound of each smack, the stifled cries of the helpless girl, and the way she squirms at each sharp spank. He especially relishes the vision of a deepening blush spreading over a pretty derriere.

Dr. Crockett finds administering the strokes to be therapeutic for him and educational for the errant probationer.

Nurse doesn't speak but her eyes avidly follow the whipping device from its downward descent to impact on the flinching globes, the flesh reddening and quivering after each strike. *This little trainee nurse has earned these stripes,* she thinks with grim satisfaction.

Dr. Crockett finishes announcing: "That's a good start for you, Probationer Kelly." He stands enjoying the view of his handiwork and is in no hurry to pull up her clothing.

In a different scenario he'd provide after-care to soothe the burn, but a sore bottom is the whole point of training. It will serve as a constant reminder to the girl to pay attention.

Finally giving her the go-ahead to dress the doctor leaves. Nurse warns Kelly that she must be punctual and grateful for the time and attention Dr. Crockett is bestowing.

Kelly's cheeks are flaming from embarrassment and Nurse smiles to herself thinking how she'll humiliate the girl with knowing looks each time Kelly bumps her backside and hisses in pain.

Returning to the Nurses' Residence that evening Kelly doesn't let on to anyone about what happened. She's tempted to confide in her closest friend but afraid word will get back to her older sister. All through her schooling Kelly was constantly reminded of *the perfection of Patricia.* No one actually made comparisons out loud, but Kelly always knew what they were thinking, and knew she fell short.

Next day she arrived at Dr. Crockett's examining room a few minutes early. Although she was reluctant to be spanked again she understood that the busy man was taking an exceptional interest in her by giving his time to help with her career.

He's a smart man with a full schedule so he must know that these lessons will help me, otherwise he wouldn't bother, she thinks. However she dreads the thought of another session with that three-tailed tawse. Checking out her backside in the full-length mirror of the shower-room Kelly wasn't surprised to see her flesh was still pink. *Considering how tender my ass feels it should have still been red!*

The end-leaf of the table is still dropped down so Kelly steps into place. She pulls her torso up towards the head of the table and lies there waiting. It's only ten minutes or so before Dr. Crockett enters the room but Kelly has fretted herself into such a state of worried anticipation that she feels like she's been there for hours.

She doesn't know that this is all part of the physician's plan. He immediately chastises her for still having all her clothes on. "Pants off!" he demands, "Quickly, quickly. You must always have your bottom bared and ready for discipline."

Blushing furiously Kelly slides her scrubs and underpants down where they fall off her legs. While she's doing that Dr. Crockett picks up his preferred spanking tool and is lightly tapping it into his palm. "You should also have this tawse out and ready for me to use, trainee."

Kelly nods her understanding of the rules. Before she even gets her fingers curled around the edge of the table the first strike falls and her hips jerk in crystal clear recall of yesterday's lesson.

The poor girl is really feeling the bite of the tails today. Dr. Crockett is pleased to notice that her flesh is still pink, she marks up so beautifully. The entertaining view of her fat little bottom shimmying and squirming invites him to take his time and do a thorough job.

Kelly's face is wet with tears by time the doctor is finished with her. Panting for air she manages to say *thank you for your time, Dr. Crockett* just as Nurse told her she should.

"I'll see you after your shift for round two, my dear. I hope you do a good job today so that you don't get spanked extra hard tonight. Nurse will keep me informed."

Kelly does feel Nurse's eye on her throughout her shift. The woman frequently – and knowingly - backs Kelly into doors and walls as well. Each contact sends a flare of pain to her eyes showing Nurse just exactly how sore Kelly is, but nothing is said.

Never a clock-watcher today Kelly can't stop checking the time. Part of her longs to get her ordeal over with while another part wishes time really could stand still. She has to seat herself gingerly at her afternoon break.

All too soon Nurse is calling "Come with me, Probationer Kelly."

Filled with trepidation the hapless girl follows. Dr. Crockett is waiting, tawse in hand, and gesturing for Kelly to climb up on the table he gives his attention to Nurse who reports *sadly, there was no improvement.*

The doctor judicially deems *it's early days, but best we begin as we mean to continue.* Shaking his head he warns Kelly that *you've earned yourself a severe correction and I hope you'll do better tomorrow.* Yanking down her clothes he begins immediately laying down rapid, powerful strokes.

This morning's spanking is still evident in the color of her cheeks and she can't keep still as she feels the bite of each sting. Soon her bottom is flaming and she's practically dancing under the whip of the wicked tails.

Under Nurse's watchful eye the doctor is forced to contain his glee *but honestly,* he thinks to himself, *this girl couldn't please me more.* Dr. Crockett is a true martinet when it comes to wayward trainees.

By Thursday Kelly is ready to call in sick. She's been spanked twice each day and her throbbing bottom is ruining her sleep. Of course she doesn't beg off. She has a job to do and must do it well or accept the consequences.

She's naked from the waist down, prone on the examining table, with the hated tawse lying beside her. Nurse no longer comes along to witness the training and Kelly is thankful to be spared that extra embarrassment of an audience to her shame. Dr. Crockett has become friendlier, or at least more chatty, now that it's just the two of them.

After greeting her *good morning* he picks up the tawse only to put it back down again explaining: "I've brought a different implement today. This will teach you the difference between a stingy versus a thuddy spanking. Both methods work wonderfully well, especially when the paddle is applied with a firm hand. The tawse uses the wrist more... but both require a strong arm."

Kelly discovers that she hates the wooden paddle just as much as the tawse. She certainly can feel the difference, but both items leave her tender and tearful. Her poor bottom feels blistered and bruised but she no longer bothers to check it out because it never looks as bad as it feels which doesn't seem right.

At the end of the day Nurse congratulates Kelly on an error-free shift. "No need to see Dr. Crockett until tomorrow morning." Kelly is thrilled to escape another lesson and equally pleased to know she's improving and not suffering through her training in vain.

Next day Dr. Crockett is also congratulatory. He tells Kelly that her morning paddling will continue for the foreseeable future, to keep her *up to par*, but he doesn't think she'll need any more after-shift refreshers.

"You've shown good results from your training and much quicker than your sister ever did. Patricia became very well-acquainted with this very same three-tailed tawse and with my wooden paddle," he confides, unwittingly shocking Kelly speechless.

Show Some Respect

The Black Death Motorcycle Club throws a wicked party. The clubhouse rings with the noise of laughter and fights, loud rock with a thumping bass, and the giggles and screams of the women who are drawn to the bad boy vibe they're guaranteed to find there. It's crowded and hot with plenty of fucking, lots of drink and drugs, and good times shared among the brothers with their guests.

The aftermath is a different story. Weak sunlight filters in through the only two windows, dirty skylights way up in the high ceiling, on to a scene of semi-nude men and women sprawled gracelessly on tables, chairs, the floor, and each other.

The stench of spilled beer, stinkweed and stale cigarette smoke, and bodies sweating out booze combines with raucous snoring and hungover moans and groans.

Vice-President Blade, feeling his almost fifty years of age in the worst way, rubs at his temple trying to erase a screaming headache. A moment ago it was only pounding but now it shrieks like... like a teenage girl throwing a hissy fit.

He's brought up sharply by the pain when he swings his head round to find the source of that tantrum. Squinting through bloodshot eyes he searches until his gaze lands on a sexy little piece wearing Daisy Dukes with a top tied under her tits to show off a flat belly.

Hands on her hips she's hollering at some poor sucker... oh yeah, it's the youngest of the Prospects called Kyle or Keegan or Kevin or some fucking "K" name, in a loud disrespectful voice. Especially when it's as early as fuck-off-o'clock in the morning after a party.

Rage surges through the old biker in a red haze and without thinking about it he's propelled himself across the room to grab hold of this irritating-as-fuck little girl.

She starts squawking *what are you*—but before she can finish that sentence he's flipped her across his lap and landed a heavy swat to her tempting rear-end. But Blade isn't thinking about how attractive those rounded globes are. No, he's thinking about teaching this spoiled little Miss a lesson on how to behave respectfully around the grown-ups.

Although half her butt is already hanging out of the cut-offs he grabs hold of the fabric and yanks hard, ripping the side seams. *Denim wouldn't have done that,* he thinks, glad the girl chose this thin stretchy fabric instead.

He continues to pull the material away from her body until her pretty little bottom is bared enticingly. It's all the invitation he needs. He starts waling on her young flesh and the result of each *smack! smack! smack!* is eminently satisfying. A flush of color appears, deepening with every stroke.

The teen screeches and howls, kicking up her heels and drumming her fists against his thigh. Blade simply swings his right leg over both of hers to keep her pinned down. She bucks her hips, futilely twisting trying to evade his hard callused palm, and the sight of her jiggling, quivering ass is a pretty picture.

Blade becomes aware that some of the others have drifted over, attracted by the *thwack* of skin striking skin and to enjoy the spectacle of a hollering girl getting *a good seeing to.*

He doesn't mind an audience *but I bet she does,* he thinks chuckling to himself. *This sure is curing my hangover headache. Good to know!*

"Nothing like a good old-fashioned walloping to keep a girlie in line," comments one brother. Another agrees and pulling on his Old Lady's ponytail tells her she's just about overdue for a lesson herself. She gives a defiant head-toss but can't disguise the light of interest that flares in her eyes.

They all return their attention to the entertaining exhibition Blade is putting on with young Keenan's girlfriend. Probably ex-girlfriend now.

He's achieved a steady rhythm applying stroke after stroke despite the girl's loud protests. She's moved from swearing and threatening to pleading and promising.

Thirty years ago I'd be tapping this hard, he thinks, *hell even twenty years ago. But now I sure as shit don't have the patience for a brat – no matter how sweet her ass glows.*

He pauses to give his handiwork consideration, trying to decide if the spanking if done, when Little Miss I-don't-know-when-to-shut-up hollers through a mouthful of tears *put me down now you old asshole!*

Looking around the ring of avid faces Blade rumbles a chuckle from deep in his chest. *This just gets better and better!* he thinks happily.

"Old, eh?" he smirks, laying down a really hard swat.

"*Old asshole,*" Diesel adds helpfully.

Nodding at his Prez Blade agrees: "Yup, there's still a whole lot of disrespect that needs to be spanked out of this cute bum. It's already red-hot but I think even an *old asshole* like me can manage to get her to fiery-hot. Maybe even blisteringly burning."

All the while he's been talking he's continued spanking back and forth on each cheek harder than before. Focusing on her tender sit spots has the girl caterwauling her grief. By now the original crowd has grown more than double in size with plenty of commentary and even a few clappers keeping the beat.

In all of her nineteen years on this earth the girl has never felt so humiliated, so degraded, so shamed... to say nothing of the throbbing, stinging agony of her poor bottom.

Her regretful apologies are noted but ignored. Blade is relentless in teaching the girl a lesson to last her a lifetime. Finished, he gives an almighty sigh as he leans back and shoves her off his lap.

She falls on her knees but is up off the floor in a flash. Keenan is there with a long hoodie to cover her up before hurrying her away.

Blade is surprised at just how much the palm of his hand burns. He wears plenty of scars along with his calluses so he can only guess how much the pain that girl is now feeling on her sensitive skin.

Deep in thought he rubs at the tingling heat while his gaze drifts through the audience until he catches the eye of Greta. She's looking from his face to his hands with blatant longing. Blade returns her lustful look with interest.

Way back when Greta was the same age as that girl today Blade fell in love with her. He never got the chance to let her know because Reaper, his best friend, claimed her first. When Reaper became Club President Margaret, Maggie as she was known to everyone else, made a great Old Lady but after her husband died she no longer came to their parties.

She'd often swing by the clubhouse next morning, just like today, to help clean up and feed the brothers. That meant Blade got to see her from time to time, but Greta always stuck close to the other Old Ladies.

Standing up Blade moves towards her with purpose. Greta doesn't back down, instead she lifts her chin to look up into his face. He realizes that Reaper's been dead several years and Greta has never shown an interest in any other man. Until now.

Heat rises through his body as he thinks how hot it would be to have Greta over his knee, wiggling her ass while he delivered a few sharp smacks. There was nothing sexy about spanking that girl, but Greta! well... he can easily picture her bare and giggling while his fingers trail down the crack of her bottom to slip in between her invitingly parted thighs.

He's stepped even closer into her personal space but she hasn't backed away. Any doubts he has are dispelled when the tip of her tongue tauntingly licks around her lips, teasing him like the brat she is and making him growl.

In His Hands

When Cesare stands and moves over to my side of the table, extending his hand to request a dance naturally I look to my father for permission.

He doesn't smile but I can tell he's pleased that I'm deferring to him. That's good. I'm never quite sure how Daddy is going to react. Usually not well so I've learned it's best to minimize and efface myself as much as possible.

Things were different when my mother was alive, she acted as a buffer between my father and the rest of the world. I don't know if it was love or sacrifice on her part... maybe a mixture of both. Now that she's gone our home feels like a minefield, ready to detonate at the slightest misstep. I move about quietly, always cautious, always on the alert, sticking to the known safe routes.

With the merest hint of a smile Daddy gestures towards Cesare saying: "Of course you can dance with your fiancé, Bella."

I nod my thanks, eyes downcast, as I allow Cesare to lead me out onto the dance floor. We're at a wedding and it seems every single person I've spoken to tonight has told me *you're next!* As if I didn't know... the arrangements were made a year ago and Cesare has patiently waited for me to come of age.

This marriage protects my father's empire and allies the Santucci family to the prestige of our name. We have history, a reputation, and a bloodline. The Santuccis have money.

Since the Santucci Don is a widower I'm lucky that my betrothed is his son and not the old man himself. Cesare has a handsome face and is only 18 years my senior.

As we dance I notice people nod in greeting but keep their distance. They might joke with me about our upcoming nuptials but no one dares to joke with my fiancé.

Cesare is tall and broad-shouldered, with an alien masculine scent I find irresistible and I inhale it deeply. When he speaks quietly I hear the rumble of his voice deep in his chest. I feel the vibration of it and look up into his face shyly but with curiosity. I've never been held in a man's arms before.

He tightens his hold pulling me even closer. I lean in wanting to hear every word that he's whispering in my ear.

"Soon you will be my wife and I won't need anyone's permission to hold your hand or dance with you or do anything I please with you."

He's smiling but there's an edginess to his tone of voice. I guess he didn't like me deferring to my father. I need to show him I'm not just a meek and mild girl.

Tilting my head I flutter my lashes at him and question: "Don't I get a say in what happens?"

His smile turns his face from handsome to gorgeous. His happy grin, accompanied by a pleasant purring growl, beams down at me. With a quick squeeze he draws me really close this time. Certain my father's eyes will be on me I try to pull back but Cesare holds me firmly in place.

Bending his head his hot breath in my ear makes me shiver. I feel hot and cold and I'm trembling. "I will never stop you from saying what's on your mind Miss Cristabella."

The momentary delight I feel is immediately quashed as he continues: "Your backtalk and sassiness will give me ample reason to thoroughly punish this delectable body."

Now I jerk back and look at him with a mixture of shock and outrage but he only chuckles. He lightly licks my ear and then murmurs his appreciation at the softness of my skin. The tremor turns a shiver into a shudder, as if he's twanging my nerve endings. I can feel a thrill of excitement ripple right through my body.

"I've been anticipating our wedding night with a great deal of pleasure, *mi piccola gattina*."

I need to resist whatever it is that his sensuous voice is doing to my insides. "*Gattina*? You should know that even kittens have claws," I retort.

Laughing he answers: "Then I will consider it my duty to de-claw you."

"That's cruel."

"Oh Bella, you must know that I'm a cruel man." Cesare has one hand at my waist and the other is holding my hand. He pulls our two hands to his chest and uses them to take hold of my chin turning my face upwards to meet his eyes.

"I will strip you and spank you and fuck you to tears. You will spend our honeymoon naked with a bright red bottom, sore nipples, and a tender pussy as I deflower your virgin body and then use it repeatedly."

I'm offended. By his words, by the fact that he dares to speak to me this way, and by my body for lighting up.

I want to fight back against his arrogance, to provoke him, so I snap: "What if I'm not a virgin?"

"If you aren't then I'll finish the fucking but the marriage will be over."

"If you f-f-fuck me," I have difficulty saying that word out loud, "you can't annul our marriage."

"No need, *gattina*. You'll be dead."

I stop in the middle of the dance floor my mouth fallen open in shock.

In a voice choked with tears I whisper: "You would kill me for that?"

"Me? no. Your father would when I returned you to him." He gives an impatient sigh at my horrified look.

"Listen up. In my position there can never be the slightest doubt about my wife's suitability. That's why I entered into this contract for a young, untouched Mafia bride, Cristabella. Is here something we need to discuss now? Before the wedding?"

My vision blurs with unshed tears as I mutely I shake my head *no*. I'm the one who's been crushed, my brief moment of defiance passed.

"Of course I'm a virgin, I've been under my father's watchful eye my entire life."

"*Piccolina*, don't be sad. I'm very happy with the arrangement our fathers made. The fact that you're beautiful is an added bonus. I plan to impregnate you as soon as possible and you will be my compliant and complacent wife.

Now I will have to discipline you for what you just said, trying to worry me," he makes a tut-tut-tut sound with his tongue. It makes me feel like a child.

"Let me think... okay, I have an idea how to... hmm, yes I'm sure I can make that happen in a day or two. You have plenty of time to anticipate the punishment that's in store for you."

Laughing he claims he's made a pun. I don't get it until he explains that he'll schedule a shopping trip and will be waiting for me in the ladies change-room of the store.

"I'll make sure it's an exclusive boutique where my money will ensure our privacy. Once I've got you alone well..." he breaks off to give me a wolfish grin. I've never been alone with a man before. This dance is the most contact I've ever had with any male. I'm holding my breath, trembling and utterly rapt, waiting to hear his next words.

I've completely forgotten my surroundings until we're heavily jostled by an inebriated couple who begin fulsome apologies until they catch the expression on Cesare's face. They immediately bow then turn away.

The way they shoved into us pushed me up close against Cesare's chest. His gravelly whisper is once again driving me to distraction.

"I will seat myself and pull you across my lap. Once I've placed you firmly over my knee I'll pull down your panties and will give you a hard spanking on your bare bottom."

I'm sure my eyes are like saucers and I know my mouth has fallen open because I can hear my panting breaths. I thought he was going to say he'd kiss me thoroughly and maybe even take liberties running his hands over my clothes. I never imagined he say this! Or that my body would respond the way it's doing, but his lips leave a trail of goosebumps where he brushes them against my throat.

24

"I'll have you squealing and wiggling and kicking your legs but I won't let up until your pretty derriere is as red as a ripe tomato. And I'll squeeze it to savor the plump juiciness of your young flesh."

Finding my voice at last I insist: "No! No, you can't do that, I won't let you."

That sets him off in a happy chuckle as he assures me he can and will turn me over his knee whenever he likes. "You will be spanked often, Bella. It's my way. You will learn your place – and be kept there - one stinging punishment at a time."

My face crumples on the verge of tears but he kisses my forehead, mindful that we're in company, and explains: "It will be my pleasure to introduce you to erotic spankings.

For truly bad behavior I'll have to take my belt to you and believe me, you'll know the difference if I ever have to welt your tender flesh. But for naughtiness I'm sure you'll find that a hand spanking from your man can be extremely arousing."

My dress is very modest with a ruched bodice to further disguise my bosom ensuring my hard, swollen nipples are hidden from view, but I'm equally sure that Cesare is well aware of the state I'm in. My throat and shoulders are in goosebumps from the thrill of his hot breath brushing over my skin, carrying his words right to my center. To say nothing of the tingling that's happening between my clenched thighs.

Cesare smirks knowingly and gives me one final squeeze before guiding me back to my father waiting at our table. As he pulls out my chair he says:

"Don, since neither Cristabella nor I have our mothers any more I'd like to arrange for one of my aunts, of course knowing them it will probably end up being two or three, take her on a shopping trip. I'd like my wedding present to be Cristabella's trousseau."

I gasp, thinking *he's going to make good on his threat to give me a sound spanking in the change-room,* and my father greets me with a suspicious look. However he only has smiles for Cesare Santucci, Mafia Prince.

25

Two days later a well-dressed matron and her daughter arrive in a town car accompanied by their bodyguards. Aunt Tonina has met my father before so they renew their acquaintance and he allows me to go shopping under her watchful eye.

During the drive to a street renowned for its exclusive designer stores I exchange pleasantries with Tonina and Alexandra, anxious to learn all I can about the family I'll be marrying into. I'm relieved to find them very friendly, open, and blunt.

"I'm afraid I never did like your father, my dear, but your mother was an absolute sweetheart. I'm so sorry for your loss, you must really miss her."

"I do, especially with this wedding coming up. We were very close although I think she sheltered me from a lot of things."

Thinking a moment Tonina nods in agreement but only says: "I'm sure she did."

We arrive at the boutique and are ushered inside with great ceremony. The Santucci wealth literally opens doors and we are served by the owner herself.

Tonina explains that we don't need the traditional trousseau of bed and bath linens since Cesare's home is already sumptuously stocked. Instead, we want to see a selection of lingerie to wear on my wedding day and for my honeymoon. I'm completely tongue-tied and grateful as Tonina smoothly takes charge.

All the fabrics are soft silk and delicate lace. Holding them in my hands I know that wearing them will make me feel absolutely beautiful. The heat rises in my cheeks as the two women gently tease me about my wedding night, and specifically about my bridegroom. I'm tempted to ask Tonina *what will happen? what can I expect?* but my shyness holds me back.

"Cesare is such a bossy man, well you'll know something about that already considering what he's arranged for today," says Tonina shaking her head but with a twinkle in her eye.

Wondering how much she knows I look around for him and there he is, lounging against the door into the change-room area. He's dressed casually in black and once I catch his eye he starts rolling up his shirt sleeves, revealing tattoos on his strong forearms.

I don't have words to describe the sensations running through me from head to toe but it's like he's got me mesmerized. When Cesare crooks a finger summoning me I'm frozen in place until Tonina gives me a little push. Then I'm drawn to him like he's a powerful magnet.

I can hear Alexandra's curious whisper and her mother making shushing noises behind me as I move towards him.

As soon as I'm within reach Cesare takes hold of my arm and pulls me into the room. It's fairly large for a change-room with mirrors on three walls and a straight-backed chair.

True to his word from the other night Cesare seats himself and without saying a thing pulls me across his knee. He shifts his legs and it feels like I'm going to tip right over until my hands reach the floor to steady myself. I'm awkwardly balanced in this position but grabbing hold of a chair leg helps. As does the firm grip Cesare's got around my middle. He finally breaks the silence and speaks in an admonishing tone:

"Although I've been looking forward to this my Bella, it's going to cost me a huge favor to Tonina for her help. And now I'm afraid your derriere is going to pay the price for incurring that debt.

You realize she's going to know what's happening in here, right? I mean there's music playing but it won't be loud enough to drown out the sound of my palm smacking your bare skin."

The thought of being overheard by his relatives and maybe the sales staff too! is too much for me. I start to struggle begging: "No, no we can't do this, you can't do this, I can't have all these people knowing—"

My words are cut off in shock when he lifts up my skirt and pulls down my panties. I can feel the air-conditioning on my exposed skin and knowing what he can see leaves me speechless. No one has ever seen me bare since I was a toddler. Not even a doctor, I've never been sick.

But once that first strike connects I can't help but yelp *ow!* Cesare only chuckles as he settles in to do a thorough job of giving me a sound spanking.

He spanks steadily up and down, left to right, fully covering all of my rear-end with his heavy hand. I sense he's holding back and thank goodness! Because the stinging burn has got me shifting from side to side in a most humiliating way.

To complete my embarrassment Cesare instructs me to look in the mirror and oh! What a sight we make. Him intent on his task, his eyes focused on my red bum, while I'm squirming in his lap shamelessly on full display.

Meeting my gaze in the mirror he winks making me close my eyes but I can't help peeking again at our reflections. My butt is nice and round and he looks at it with real pleasure.

After an eternity or so Cesare stops spanking me and announces: "I won't touch your little pussy, I'm content to wait until we're married, but since it's bare and exposed I'm certainly going to take a good look. I am your fiancé, after all."

He parts my thighs and mortifies me further by making complimentary *mmm-mmm* sounds. Then he leans in and inhales - noisily! I feel awful but then he groans and it sounds very uh... um... well, hot so I don't complain.

The mirror displays the lust in his eyes as he holds me down while taking his time to gaze at my private place. I twitch a couple of times because it's impossible to keep still. Not when he's staring at me like that.

Finally he rights my clothing and lifts me to my feet. I guess it shows that I'm ashamed and unhappy because he speaks quite seriously when he says: "Bella, you are perfection. I want to be a good husband to you and I'm hoping we can have something more than a marriage of convenience for the benefit of our families. If you can learn my lessons and bow to my will I'm certain we'll find happiness. Are you willing to try?"

He looks so earnest that I find my trembling lip forming a small smile as I agree. I've always known what role I was born to fulfill, I truly am a Mafia Princess.

Alternative Therapy

"Looking back, to your earliest memories, what is the first spanking-related incident that comes to mind?" His voice is deep and melodious, compelling me to answer.

Sitting in the waiting room before my appointment I had second thoughts about trying this new therapy. Then I met the psychologist who, although considerably older than me, is still panty-melting gorgeous. A true *silver fox.*

A very vivid recollection immediately fills my head-space at his question but I'm not sure it's the right answer. Hesitantly I begin: "It wasn't me being spanked.." and let my voice trail off.

The expression on his face only shows polite encouragement, but he eyes me for a long moment before gesturing that I should continue.

"I was four years old. I know that because we lived in an apartment that year, far from our own home. My parents rented out our house because all the families in the construction crew were given accommodation while the workers put up the buildings.

I was at a neighbor's playing with the boy who was my age or maybe a bit younger. I never saw if what he did was an accident or deliberate, but suddenly I heard a crash and there was his mother's treasured snow globe lying shattered on the floor.

I knew it happened because I was talking to his mother, but whether he was jealous of her attention or mine I have no idea. Maybe it wasn't jealousy, maybe he was just distracted, but regardless of why he dropped the ornament he was going to get punished.

His mother reminded him that he wasn't allowed to touch that globe *as you very well know!* I remember that she was really angry, it showed in her face and I could hear it in her voice.

She pulled him across her lap and he started crying loudly before she even got his corduroy trousers pulled down. Along with his underpants.

He was scared of getting spanked, plus he clearly didn't like having his bottom bared in front of me, but she wasn't listening to him.

I can very clearly see her hand sharply striking his small bottom as it blossomed pinker and pinker. He pummeled his fists and kicked his feet in a real tantrum, screeching all the while.

But as the spanking continued he stopped yelling and started pleading. His skin turned red and his cries were frantic so obviously it was a painful punishment. I guess she took her temper out on him.

I have no idea how long it lasted, I simply stood staring transfixed. I think the mother had forgotten I was there. She looked up and ordered me to *go home, now!* and I didn't hesitate to hurry out the door.

I turned for one last look at them and saw him standing clutching her legs and sobbing into her lap *I'm sorry, Mommy* while she stroked his hair.

I wish I'd looked at her face to see what expression she was wearing but I was too afraid to linger a second longer."

What feels like a lengthy silence follows my recitation. Half of my mind is still back in that apartment while grown-up me is trying to figure out if the psychologist can decipher some meaning in this tale.

Eventually he smiles at me in an encouraging way. "Tell me, were you ever spanked yourself?"

"Sort of..." I laugh at how foolish I sound. "One time I wandered off and was found by a neighbor who rushed me back home, we were back living in our own house then, and I didn't know why there were all these people gathered but it turns out my mother had called the police.

Anyhow, she started swatting my backside, over my clothes, while crying *I'm so glad you're home, I so glad you were found* and that stuck with me because it was such an odd reaction. That's the only corporal punishment I can ever recall receiving."

"Interesting that you say *corporal punishment* instead of *spanking*. It sounds like you think swats on your clothed backside don't constitute an actual, or maybe more factually a *real* spanking."

I don't know how to answer so I study my nails while waiting for him to go on. He surprises me by chuckling and when my head jerks up I see real mirth in the look he gives me.

"It believe you think a proper spanking has to be administered over-the-knee on a bare bottom, correct?"

I don't answer in words but to my shame he notices me squirming in reply. I force myself to stay still and ignore the heat of a blush rising up. That just makes his eyes twinkle with merriment.

If only he had a big stomach and a full white beard I could pretend he was a man dressed up as Santa Claus but instead he's well-built and attractive and his eyes are so blue and the look he's giving me is spellbinding.

"As you know from the questionnaire you completed online before we scheduled this appointment one of the main therapies I use in this practice is physical discipline. The form that takes varies from patient to patient, depending on their... needs.

I propose we complete today's session with *a good old-fashioned bare-bottomed spanking.* Ah yes," he remarks in a pleased tone of voice, "that phrase has triggered your pupils to dilate and your breathing to shallow denoting an increased heart rate."

Nodding in satisfaction he lays his notepad down on the end-table and patting his knee indicates I should place myself across his lap. My insides are flip-flopping and my mind is a jumble thinking *do I want this? yes, but why? what am I doing?*

Without realizing it I've gotten to my feet and am standing before him wordlessly. He takes my arm and guides me into position. His no-nonsense manner is weirdly reassuring as he reaches round to unbutton and unzip my jeans before pulling them down my legs. I deliberately wore blue jeans for the protection of the thick denim but I'm not getting any say in this.

My panties are dragged along with them and when I automatically try to grab hold he captures my hand and places it securely at the small of my back. I'm immediately self-conscious about being half-naked with this stranger.

Yet I feel a shivery thrill of anticipation for my spanking mixed with some fear that it will hurt. *Of course it will hurt, idiot!* I tell myself. *His heavy hand is going to strike your tender behind over and over again so yeah, it's going to be painful.* But that tinge of fear only adds to my excitement.

In a matter-of-fact voice he begins reprimanding me about being *a naughty girl for avoiding the sound spanking you so richly deserve.* He's smacking my bum hard and it really stings! Each strike is loud and though I try to keep silent I can't help the embarrassing gasps and yelps that escape me.

My tormentor just keeps patterning my flesh with his handprints. He makes sure to cover the whole area. I feel a sharp pain from the top of my crack down over the fleshy mounds to the curve of my sit-spots and the top of my thighs. This isn't role-playing therapy, this is a serious spanking. I'm being punished hard for real!

Shamefully I feel myself squirming and squealing but he simply continues each rhythmic *smack-smack-smack* ignoring my humiliating display. He stops and rests his palm on my sore flesh as if testing the warmth then he murmurs something to himself and resumes spanking.

"You need to know there's a firm hand ready to correct your missteps, little one. To keep you in line being a good girl, and to discipline your naughty bottom when you stray."

As he says that something breaks loose inside of me releasing pent-up feelings I couldn't put into words if I tried. Instead there's an easing and the freedom to let loose with deep sobbing.

I feel him gently massaging my sore behind and I think I can hear him humming. If so, it's a very low sound. Soothing. After awhile he helps me to stand and I pull up my clothes. I feel completely at ease and face him without any embarrassment. I'm not ashamed of my tears or about being disciplined by this man, in fact it all feels so very right.

34

Swallowing deeply I knuckle the tears from my face and look him in the eye. Whatever he sees gives him the answer he wants and he nods in satisfaction.

"You won't have to return for some time my dear, but when you feel the need just schedule a visit online. Also... your bottom is lovely and plump so I'd like to try a nice hard-backed wooden hairbrush next time. Think it over, okay?"

Oh this man... he knows damn well I won't be able to think of anything else!

A Semi-Public Punishment

Rick and his college buddies remain good friends long after graduation. They don't live near each other, but still manage to keep in touch frequently.

Rick was all set to propose to Tiffany, the girl he's crazy about, but he caught her messing around with her coworker. *Not fucking, but kissing and groping,* he told his friends.

The men all agree that Rick should *kick her to the curb* but they can see he's utterly gutted without her. And Tiffany is tearfully promising it will never happen again and wants him back.

Rick is torn. He truly loves Tiffany but feels he can't trust her so how can he possibly forgive and forget? His friends suggest he give her a memorable and meaningful punishment. Something that - if she agrees to it - will prove her devotion to Rick.

"What do you mean?" he asks, sounding hopeful for the first time since his heartbreaking discovery.

"Well, something that humiliates her, that shows her you're the boss, and that she's damn lucky to have you."

"Like what?"

His still-single friend says: "Deep-throat her, but in a really mean way. Fuck her mouth hard, barely letting up so she's gasping for air and then cum all over her face. She'll be crying and drooling and covered in cum that you'll make her wipe off with her fingers and then lick them clean."

"Jesus Kyle, did you see that on a porno?"

"Never mind how I know, just believe me I can guarantee that degradation is effective."

Harry interrupts excitedly to say: "But first get her to give you a lap dance that she's got to make really slutty. I mean wagging her tongue and moaning and spreading her butt-hole and twerking.

Oh and tell her she can't touch you but she has to touch herself, to rub her little clit until she's ready to orgasm and then make her stop. Do that a couple of times until she's practically crying and begging to cum. Then face fuck her like Kyle said."

"Yeah, definitely do both those things," agrees Marcus, "but after you've cum and she hasn't put her across your knee and spank her hard. Just wale on that ass until it's red-hot and she's screaming and creaming for you."

There's a momentary silence on the phone while the four men consider this picture in their minds' eye.

Finally Rick answers: "Oh yeah, that sounds really good. If she's willing to do all that then I'll believe she is remorseful and means it when she promises to be faithful and behave herself."

"Oh and for the humiliation part? You do it all on video chat and let her know that we'll be watching her every move and judging her sincerity," states Marcus.

Harry intervenes saying: "Maybe Rick doesn't want us to see her naked, I mean if they do end up getting married—"

"Shut the fuck up, Harry!" interrupts Kyle.

Rick replies: "No, funny enough I'm okay with it. I know you guys don't think I should be giving her a second chance but believe me once you see her in the flesh you'll understand. And you guys, well... it's all cool."

"Good, I mean I wouldn't have suggested that if I thought you'd have a problem with it, man. You know I think most women are exhibitionists deep down, anyhow. But whether she is or isn't I'm sure that being ordered around by you while she's naked in front of your friends has definitely got to be embarrassing."

"And Rick don't approach Tiffany, wait until she calls or texts you again. Make it seem like you're doing her a favor by letting her *apologize* this way."

The friends all agree with this advice and encourage their buddy to *stay strong*.

Rick doesn't have to wait long until he hears from Tiffany again, pleading with him to take her back. He offers to meet her, not wanting to discuss the proposal by text or call, and suggests her place so he can leave when he wants. Tiffany is delighted he's coming over.

When Rick arrives he can smell his favorite food, lasagne, baking in the oven. Following her into the living room he sees a good red wine set out to breathe and hears instrumental music playing low. The only lighting comes from aromatherapy candles creating a romantic atmosphere.

Tiffany's face falls when Rick tells her he isn't hungry and won't be staying long enough to have a drink. Instead he lays out the proposed punishment to prove her claim that she truly is repentant.

Tiffany is reluctant, feeling shy and ashamed to be naked and performing sexually in front of his friends, but in the end she accepts. Rick sighs heavily pretending he's not convinced this will be enough, but it's an ordeal he'll power through.

They schedule her session at his apartment this coming Friday, three days from now, giving both of them plenty of time to anticipate. He tells her to wear *that red slip dress with nothing else except high-heels*.

When he gets up to go Tiffany presses her warm, voluptuous body tight against him. Her gaze is inviting, and her perfume seductive, so he has to struggle to remember his friends' advice to stay strong, but he manages to leave without another word.

On Friday night the ambience of Rick's home is anything but romantic. All the lights are on, and there's no food, no drink, and no music. He's dressed casually in jeans and a t-shirt. He didn't shave that morning and his stubbly chin gives him an intimidating look that fits with the air of menace he projects.

He's chosen the living room so there's plenty of space for Tiffany to perform. The coffee table has been cleared off for her to lie on, and he's positioned his iPad so his friends have the same unobstructed view he'll get watching her from his armchair.

Tiffany arrives about ten minutes early and her anxiety level is already pitched high. Her eyes are bright and her skin is flushed. Stepping through the door she reaches up to give Rick a kiss but he pulls back and simply takes her coat without a word.

She's wearing the red dress. It's very short at the bottom and very low-cut at the top with only thin straps to hold it up. Tiffany has a full, womanly shape. Heavy breasts, sagging a bit without a bra, wide hips, a bit of a belly, and a plump heart-shaped ass.

"Stand here," Rick says, placing Tiffany in front of the iPad. "My friends want to meet you."

Tiffany turns to look at the screen but the audience have turned off their cameras so all she sees are names and avatar placeholders. They've kept their audio on though and she can hear them talking with each other asking *is this the slut who cheated on Ricky?* and making comments of *a bit fatter than I normally like* and *nice rack, though.*

Her glance drifts towards Rick but he's no help, he simply announces *this is Tiffany* and cueing up music on his phone "Tears" by Sabrina Carpentar starts playing.

"Give me a striptease, Tiffany," he orders. "Convince me you're a horny slut hungry for my cock but remember you can't touch it."

Tiffany has been practising at home in front of her mirror. She didn't know what tune Rick would choose but knows it doesn't matter because it isn't her dancing he's interested in.

No, he wants to see me acting like a whore, and putting on a show for his friends, she acknowledges to herself.

Undulating sinuously Tiffany runs her hands down the length of her mini-dress, caressing her body. She plays with the hem, swinging it, then spinning with it raised to give him a glimpse of bare pussy and ass-cheeks.

Then she cups her breasts through the material before squeezing and rotating them roughly, all the while licking her tongue around her open mouth.

Reaching up she slides the spaghetti straps of her dress over her shoulders. Shimmying her torso the bodice of her dress ripples down until it catches on her nipples, erect enough to poke the silky material and hold it up.

Pushing her palms in from each side she mashes her breasts together before thrusting them forward in offering. One of the men calls out: "Pull on those nipples and twist them. Show my boy Rick just how sorry you are."

Tiffany blushes but follows the instructions with a sexy pout. She continues to dance, easing the dress over her hips that she rotates slowly. Turning all the way around everyone gets a good look as her body is fully bared. Still wearing her heels she steps out of the dress.

"Now twerk for me, Tiffany," Rick orders.

She squats and lift her hips but stops, suddenly self-conscious at having her private parts exposed to strangers.

"Now, slut!" he barks out the command and Tiffany starts swiveling her hips before jerking up and down, flashing her bare pussy at both Rick and the video cam.

"Oh yeah, just like that baby," one voice calls. Another cheers her on to *shake that booty*.

Tiffany spends several minutes clenching and jiggling her butt cheeks, anxious about how wobbly her bottom looks, before turning back again and dancing her way over to Rick.

Holding the arms of his chair she leans over caging him in with her full breasts swinging inches from his face.

Reaching up Rick cruelly flicks first one nipple then the next making Tiffany squeak. He smirks and does it again then repeats the action several more times while she just has to hang over him accepting the painful torment. Her nipples are fully distended and a red flush radiates out over her breasts.

"Lie back on the coffee table and put each foot up here, where your hands were," he says patting the chair's padded arms. Tiffany positions herself and he moves the stool holding the iPad asking *is everybody able to get a good look at this cunt?*

"Oh yeah, it's a pretty one," comments one friend. "Is she always hairless or did you order her to wax or whatever it is they do?"

"I ordered a bare snatch since I wanted us all to get a clear view. She usually has something different done each time: landing strips or little tufts of curls... you like showing off your pussy to me, don't you slutty girl?"

She bites her lip and nods while one of the men chuckles adding: "For the rest of my life any time someone mentions Tiffany this is the picture I'll see in my mind before I remember what her face looks like."

Tiffany's pink blush deepens to a rosy red. She glances down but Rick says: "Uh-uh whore, eyes on me, own your shame."

Enhancing the punishment they'd originally agreed on Rick tells Tiffany to massage her tits while he abuses her clit with a *magic wand*. Three times he brings her to the very edge of ecstasy before pulling back until her arousal subsides.

Tiffany knows she's squirming like the world's neediest tramp in front of Rick's friends, but she can't help moaning and mewling with lust and disappointment.

Now that her body is flushed with thwarted desire, and her breasts heave with her panting, he points to the ground telling her to *kneel, hands behind your back, while I fuck your face.*

Rick began this evening playing a part, but seeing his Tiffany naked and begging has him rock-hard. He's deeply aroused and enjoying the unexpected pleasure he's getting from punishing his naughty, unfaithful girl.

The sight of tears streaming down her face while her lips are stretched taut around his cock is entrancing. He roughly thrusts over her tongue and down her throat despite the gagging noises she's making. Rick only pulls back long enough to let Tiffany suck in a mouthful of air when her face turns red.

Dominating her with his anger as he plunges his cock into her hot wetness fulfills a primal need. Pulling out to finish he shoots his stream across her face.

When she's dripping in his cum Rick takes her hands and rubs them in the fluid before thrusting her fingers in her mouth ordering her to suck them clean. She's a stunning hot mess obediently following his every instruction.

"Stand up and lean forward to put your hands on your knees. Stick your ass out." Tiffany complies and Rick surveys her in this position for a moment before gesturing for her to turn halfway. He moves around to stand on her far side.

"Guys, have you got a good side-view so you can see her tits swing with every strike?"

The men answer in the affirmative.

When Rick tells Tiffany to arch your back and one of his friends wolf-whistles calling *tits and ass, yum-yum* her eyes widen and she has to press her lips tight together to hold in her whimpers.

Rick is relishing his role and now improvises with the original plan. He unbuckles his belt and slowly draws it through the loops of his jeans before carefully folding it in half. Tiffany is mesmerized by his actions, her eyes never leaving his hands.

Coming close Rick places his left hand on the small of her back and with his right he gives a mighty swing lashing the belt across her butt. Her whole body jumps, tits bouncing and ass jiggling, but he keeps her in place.

Oh owwwie one of the watchers breathes while another announces *that's one.*

Rick whips her with the belt again and again. She can no longer stifle her cries at each painful bite of the leather. Every stroke leaves a pink stripe on her wiggling bottom and the audience is counting along.

He's holding back, not even hitting her with half his strength, but Tiffany is quaking in anticipation of the next strike.

"One more with the belt and then you're going over my knee for the final punishment."

The sixth stroke lands with a loud *crack* and Tiffany gives out a high-pitched scream. Rick takes hold of her hips and turns her backwards to the camera to show his friends the red welts on her bum.

Seating himself he pulls her down to lay across his lap. Her round bottom is aching and throbbing when Rick lands the first spank to a resounding *one!* from their three-man audience.

"Count along, slut and be ready to thank me when I'm done."

Each forceful smack jolts Tiffany against Rick's cock and she's soon squirming to rub even harder. Trying to stimulate her clit distracts her from the burning pain of this hand-spanking on top of the belting.

After a dozen hard hits the consensus is *she needs a dozen more.*

"No! Please, please no more," a tearful Tiffany begs but Rick listens to his friends and continues with vigor. Each stinging slap has Tiffany first squealing then sobbing, but her man is relentless.

The friends see that Rick is truly ridding himself of his pent-up anger on Tiffany's very-inviting derriere. They know that painful as this vengeance might be it's a spanking, not a beating, and there's no permanent damage. Although Tiffany will certainly wear the marks and feel the effects for several days.

Especially after they unanimously agree that *yes, you need to dispense another dozen.*

Tiffany's screams are frantic and she's given up trying to count as more strokes land on her tender bottom. The heat travels to her core and her thighs fall open showing the glisten on her slit.

She's shimmying her hips from both pain and lust, and she has no idea exactly what it is that she's begging for. Rick lays a palm on her burning flesh and announces that *she's blisteringly hot.*

"Good job, man. Does it feel like she's atoned for her misbehavior?" asks Marcus.

Before Rick can answer Kyle opines: "I think it's a good start, but she's gonna need a few more sessions across your lap in the near future. You know, to totally drive the lesson home."

"I second that!" confirms Harry.

"And I can personally testify that OTK refreshers help concentrate the female mind wonderfully," Marcus puts in with a complacent chuckle.

Rick grins at the enthusiasm of his friends and lifts Tiffany so that she's kneeling on his lap with her legs spread wide. He shoves the stool back with his foot and the guys confirm that *her bright red ass is on display.*

"Tell me Tiffany, do you feel like you've been thoroughly punished? Are you penitent and sorry and deeply ashamed of yourself?"

"Yes Rick, my behind really hurts, and I feel so bad about everything. I am so-so-so sorry and I'm begging you to please forgive me."

He asks: "Do you want me to fuck you now? with the guys watching us, Tiff?"

Chewing on her bottom lip she hesitates but her needy desire has her saying: "Whatever you want Rick, I'll do anything you want."

As the fucking changes to lovemaking each of the friends click off their machines to give the gratefully reunited couple privacy.

Accepting Her Role

When the curtain drops for the third time Antonia sighs deeply. The whispers and sidelong glances of her fellow cast members mean her husband has arrived backstage. The final curtain call means she can't avoid him any longer.

His immense wealth coupled with dark stories of shady dealings make him a person of interest and gossip. But everyone wisely keeps their distance, simply sharing rumors of this dangerous man.

Antonia looks down at all the floral tributes on the stage floor, more than she can carry with her arms already full of bouquets, and knows each gift has earned her a punishment.

Even these dethorned roses come with a sharp sting, she muses looking at all the lovely flowers with regret.

Stuart is a jealous man who subjects his wife to controlled violence. He enjoys it and she chooses to stay in the marriage although neither of them know why, exactly. They've been together for many years now... it must be their version of true love.

Holding her head high to avoid the pitying looks Antonia slowly walks down the corridor to her dressing-room. As the star of the show she has her own private quarters.

At times like these that's a shame, she thinks ruefully. *Safety in numbers and all that...*

Of course Stuart is already waiting inside, reading the congratulatory cards from friends and fans that cover her make-up table. She takes a moment to study his reflection in the mirror and marvels yet again at how such a handsome, stately exterior can contain such a crazy devil.

It was Stuart's devastating good looks that drew Antonia to him long ago. Back when both of them were stage actors. Stuart was good, but he had no ambition to be famous. His quest for riches and power was found in the criminal enterprise he joined. Now he's become pretty much untouchable.

Their eyes meet in the mirror. Hers plead for mercy but his already burn with rage. Reading aloud from one of the greeting cards his vitriolic rendering turns the words sour.

"*With love and adoration from your most devoted fan, Janet Cushing.* Huh! that's a fake name if I've ever heard one. Who is he? Hmm? Is *Janet* really James? or Jake? or John?"

Then he slaps her across the face with the prettily wrapped posy of colorful pansies and daisies. It's painless but shameful. The petals fly off in every direction and quite a few stick to her skin.

Stuart pulls the boudoir chair away from table and orders her to *strip and kneel on this, so-called wife.*

Antonia would like to take off her stage make-up and the foliage but Stuart is too impatient to wait. *Plus, he likes to see my face messed up with streaks of color from my tears,* she acknowledges to herself.

Removing her costume as quickly as she can while still being careful with the garment she needs to wear again tomorrow Antonia is soon standing in her underwear. It's plain, utilitarian and white. She knows wearing sexy lingerie in sheer fabrics and lace would be like waving a red flag at a bull.

Stuart gestures for her to remove her bra then glares as her large breasts swing free. She leaves her panties on knowing that pulling them down is his job. He likes to make a production out of it.

"Get up on the chair and hold onto the back. I've got a new toy to try out."

He pulls an item from inside his suit jacket and she sees that it's a loop of plastic or maybe rubber? attached to a handle. "It's a *Loopy!*" he declares.

Antonia's eyes widen as he whisks this new implement in the air a few times. The faint hissing sound it makes fills her with dread yet it's such an innocuous-looking thing.

"It doesn't seem like much but it's very popular. It's easy to carry, guaranteed to be extra stingy, and it's silent. You won't be, but perhaps your fellow actors will think I'm fucking the screams out of you?" he chuckles with a wolfish grin.

"I'm told it will mark you like a whip and your bottom will color up to a fiery red in no time. I was promised that it will really hurt. A proper punishment for a whore."

"Stuart I am not a whore, I am your wife and I am faithful. I have always been faithful to you. We've talked about this how many times?"

His dilated pupils, turning his eyes black, answer for him. It's useless to try to communicate because Stuart is unreachable in the dark recesses of his own mind.

With the first strike Antonia sucks in a deep breath to hold back her cry. Her husband's new toy is wickedly painful. Her whole body quakes and trembles between blows making her struggle to remain in position.

Stuart grabs a fistful of her hair pulling it to hold her upright. When she protests he flicks the *Loopy* across her breasts and she does scream loudly at the bite on her tender nipples. So he does it again.

Stuart's taunting affability has now vanished and his bitter jealousy is in control. His words lash her as sharply as the whip while he hisses accusations of cheating and degrading insults of *unfaithful slut* and *greedy whore.*

The implement moves silently. It's only Stuart's diatribe that warns of an incoming strike. Right-to-left, immediately followed by left-to-right.

"How many bouquets of slutty red roses?" Slash, slash.

"I suppose that standing ovation made you think you're special?" Slash, slash.

Antonia clenches her fists and bears down on the pain. It really is excruciating and her poor bottom throbs and aches. This is her worst punishment ever and when he moves down to the tops of her thighs she starts shaking uncontrollably.

Sometimes, quite often actually, Stuart's over-the-knee spankings smart but arouse her when he caresses the marks he's made. The feel of his large hand gently stroking her pink flesh as he murmurs *naughty darling girl* is stimulating and leads to hot sex.

This is something else entirely. The new play is a huge success and Antonia has garnered rave reviews for her performance. All of that adulation has brought out the beast in Stuart.

Over and over again he strikes until he's whipped her bottom raw. He only stops when he realizes Antonia can hardly breathe through her flood of tears and choking sobs. Lifting her in his arms he cuddles her on his lap, massaging comforting circles on her back. His hand moves to her backside and the heat coming off her skin surprises and fascinates him.

When her crying jag ends he takes hold of her chin and looks searchingly into her eyes. Make-up ruined by mucus and tears has made a mess of her face and he gives a satisfied nod while she hiccups. Her eyes continue to stream but he wipes her nose and chin.

Then, with a cruel smile, he warns: "I'm not done yet."

Antonia jumps to her feet and grabbing hold of the *loopy* flings it across the room. She faces Stuart with hands fisted and her facial expression battling between fear and defiance. His is alight with an unholy grin.

"Oh my bratty darling... you will pay extra for that!" he purrs with a wicked smirk. Antonia turns to run but Stuart easily catches hold of her and flings her down on the couch.

Penning her in he strokes his fingers down the length of her naked body until he reaches between her thighs. "Now your poor pussy is going to get bitten by my new toy."

"NO! Stuart, no! It's a horrible thing and... and... it will damage me."

"Oh wife, you already are so deeply damaged... what are a few more bruises and scars on your black, corrupted soul?"

In a surprising show of strength Antonia shoves against him and draws herself up to a sitting position. "I'm not the one with the debauched and depraved soul, *husband*."

50

Roughly pushing her back down Stuart growls: "Maybe not yet... but I'm dragging you along when I go to hell." He stands up and with a deadly whisper of *don't you dare move* he freezes her into place while he retrieves the whippy implement.

She cringes away from him as crowds her against the back of the couch. Balancing on the edge he leans in, looming over her with a menacing scowl, but he's almost gentle as he flicks the *loopy* lightly over her hairless mons.

Stuart carefully watches the results and it takes less than two minutes for his wife to cry and writhe from the accumulated burn of the stingy punishment.

"Please stop, please! It really hurts, Stuart."

This time he doesn't cuddle her in his arms, instead he drops to his knees and soothes her painful red skin with tender kisses and blowing cooling breaths.

Then he licks her into a state of mindless pleasure and when she's almost crested the wave of ecstasy he pulls back and says: "Now I'm done."

Perfect Prefect

Everyone knows that Gillian's determination to be the best Prefect the Sixth Form of St Margaret's has ever known means she's overzealous and ever-vigilant.

She takes her duty to maintain order and discipline seriously so when someone starts pilfering trifles she feels it as a personal affront.

Nothing of value has been taken, but the girls have been inconvenienced by a sewing kit vanishing, a manicure set gone missing, and treats from home having disappeared.

Since no one has come forward to confess or tattle Gillian has a surprise inspection planned for tonight. When she makes the announcement the girls all exclaim at the invasion of privacy while protesting their innocence.

Nancy Harrigan is spotted slinking along the outskirts of the circle and when caught out she explains she wanted a private word with Gillian. "But since you insist, well, I'm pretty sure I saw Candace hiding something in her drawer."

As all the girls turn to look at her Candace loudly exclaims: "Me? I did no such thing. Have a look and see for yourselves!"

Leveling a stern look at the girl Gillian searches for hints of guilt and sees nothing. Nevertheless she begins her inspection by pulling open the drawer of Candace's combination dresser/desk.

Adelaide's loud cry of "Oh! Those are my mother's walnut brownies!" has everyone crowding in for a closer look. Sure enough, there's a cellophane-wrapped box of the homemade chocolate treats.

Candace's shrill cry of *I've never seen that before in my life!* is drowned out by her form-mates shouting *Thief!* and *Candace did it!* and *it's been Candace all along.*

"You're caught red-handed Candace Abernathy and now you're getting a red bottom as punishment!" declares Gillian. Turning to her charges she shouts "Grab her and bend her over this desk."

Eager volunteers latch on to the girl and overcome her struggles. Candace is soon positioned with her sleep shorts pulled down and her bare bottom poised for a thorough paddling.

Gillian wields the wooden-backed hairbrush with the same determination she shows on the field hockey team. The room is utterly quiet except for the *Thwack! Thwack! Thwack!* of each well-placed smack.

Candace is completely helpless since her form-mates have her securely pinned into place. Her exposed backside flinches as she endures every painful stroke. Her captors feel no pity, only righteous satisfaction that the thief is getting her just reward.

When Candace's poor bottom achieves the promised bright red coloring she loses her stoic silence in a loud wail of agony. Moments later the door is flung open and an angry Matron appears.

"What is the meaning of this noise?" she asks, then seeing that Candace is being held down by her dorm-mates Matron's voice thunders out *let that poor child go!*

Candace runs into Matron's comforting embrace and is hugged for a minute before being sent to the bathroom to apply some aloe gel to her flaming skin.

"Gillian you better have a very good reason for administering such a painful and humiliating public discipline to young Candace."

Gillian is ready to defend her actions but seeing how the other girls all look down, some even shuffling away, she starts to wonder *did I maybe go too far?*

Upon hearing all the commotion the Headmistress herself arrives in the Sixth Form's dormitory.

"I've just seen Candace Abernathy crying her eyes out and no wonder, the poor girl's bottom has been sorely abused."

"She stole!" bursts out Gillian. "I found the food gift Adelaide's mother sent her away hidden in Candace's drawer."

"Hmm, and was it well-hidden?"

"No, she left it right on top - plain as day!"

"And what did Candace say when you questioned her?"

In a scornful voice Gillian says: "She denied it, of course."

"And what proof do you have against Candace? Apart from finding the food?"

"Nancy saw her put it there!" concludes Gillian triumphantly.

Now all eyes turn to Nancy, the snitch, who backtracks saying: "I never said I saw her put the brownies there, just that I saw her put something away."

Matron shakes her head sadly at Gillian. "This is very disappointing. You jumped to conclusions without all the facts. I understand that it might have seemed to be *an open-and-shut case,* and that you're eager to prove yourself in this position, but a cooler head would have come to an entirely different conclusion.

The punishment you bestowed far exceeded your authority, Gillian."

"That's right!" shouts Candace from the doorway. "I'm innocent! You didn't give me a chance, none of you did." Her tear-streaked face and sob-thickened voice indicate how badly she's been physically and emotionally hurt.

The Headmistress and Matron exchange a silent communication before nodding decisively.

Matron says: "Now you'll have to be punished, Gillian, and just as publicly as poor Candace was. Take up the same position she was in. I expect that you, as a Prefect, will show some decorum. No one will hold you down, you will submit to your spanking with humility."

Frustrated, angry tears spring to Gillian's eyes but she refuses to cry in front of the Sixth Form. She places herself over the desk as indicated and waits, hoping against hope that she'll be allowed to keep her pajamas on. She is sadly disappointed.

Matron's voice is cold as she commands: "Bare your bottom for my paddle, Gillian."

The girl sucks in a deep breath recalling from an experience in her first year just how painful a session with that leather paddle can be.

Matron never holds back and she doesn't spare Gillian in the least little bit now.

Aiming low with a strong upwards swing Matron applies stroke after stroke starting at Gillian's tender sit spot and moving up to the fleshiest part of her bottom.

That earlier spanking wasn't embellished in Gillian's memory, this paddling is just as painful.

The cracking sound of leather against bare flesh echoes in the room, the only voice being Matron's as she lambastes Gillian for failing in her duty, for disappointing the staff, for harming an innocent girl, and for bringing shame on herself.

Gillian desperately tries to maintain her dignity but she can't contain her grunts and then her whimpers as Matron punishes her thoroughly with a lengthy spanking.

By the time Gillian's bottom is fully covered with red paddle-shaped patches loud sobs escape her. Her sense of decorum is completely lost as she begs for her paddling to end.

Breathing heavily from her exertion Matron finishes but keeps Gillian exposed and on display as a lesson to them all about the abuse of power.

Finally the Headmistress announces: "Now it's time to punish the real culprit. As I'm sure you've all figured out that is Nancy Harrigan.

She hid the incriminating evidence in the most convenient spot, the drawer beside her own, the drawer belonging to Candace Abernathy. Then Nancy pointed the finger appointing blame and you are all guilty of acting on her lie without clemency or mercy.

Nancy, you will now receive a hard lashing from my belt."

Nancy fights and cries but she is subdued by Matron who holds her down. The Headmistress lifts Nancy's nightie and pulls down her underpants exposing her naked backside for everyone to see.

They all notice the angry red pimple on the sit spot of her left cheek. It somehow makes Nancy seem even more vulnerable. The girls hold their breath knowing they'll be witnessing a most severe correction.

Folding her narrow belt in half the older woman proceeds to slash the leather against the girl's tender flesh raising welt after painful welt. Nancy is howling from the first strike but the Headmistress doesn't hesitate to deliver a full dozen blows.

"Three strokes for stealing, three for lying, and six for trying to shift the blame on to an innocent girl."

Nancy is graceless, bawling and shrieking, kicking out her legs. The angry red stripes stand out starkly against the pale flesh of her backside. Beads of blood form on one that was crisscrossed and the belt soon smears the red stain.

All the girls know Nancy deserves the pain but no one really approves because they're feeling remorseful for the part they played in Candace's wrongful punishment.

It's a subdued group of teenagers who take to their beds that night. Most of them are kept awake replaying the images of squirming bare bottoms getting redder and redder, and hearing the cries of girls their own age receiving hard, painful spankings.

Three of them have to lie on their stomachs, sobbing into their pillows, until they fall asleep.

His Birthday Present

"You're the hardest person in the world to buy for!" Lizzie declares.

Smirking, Andrew replies: "So I've been told."

"Well, I found something for your birthday, but I have no idea if you'll like it. It's a bit... well, unusual. I got it at that decrepit old antique shop on Church Street. Not the smart shop that nobody can afford but the one further down, looks more like used buy-and-sell goods rather than antiques, you know the one I mean?"

Andrew nods his head claiming *I'm intrigued* but looking wary. It's a dingy, dirty store with its bow-window full of dusty goods covered in cobwebs. He can't imagine any suitable gift that Lizzie could find for him in there.

"Anyhow, he called it a *conversation piece* and I know your penchant for oddities so I bought it. No refunds so now it's yours even if you hate it."

She lifts her chin looking defiant and Andrew's interest is definitely piqued. Lizzie leads the way down the hall until she reaches Andrew's combined office and library.

"Jenkins helped me put it in here but you can move it wherever you like. It's bulky rather than heavy. Anyhow, here it is," and opening the door she sweeps her arm towards the gift she's bought for her friend's fortieth birthday.

It's an oddly-shaped wooden chair upholstered in leather. A thoroughly well-worn piece of furniture, shiny from age but spotlessly clean, built sturdily to last.

Shocked, Andrew exclaims: "You got me a spanking chair! Lizzie how... how on earth did you find this? These chairs are so rare and... oh my dear, what a wonderful present! I love it."

Surprised and pleased Lizzie grins stating: "I can't believe you know what it is! I'd never heard of such a thing and the old shopkeeper was very coy about it, first calling it a spanking chair then *a correction chair* and later on *the disciplinarian's seat.*"

"Yes, of course, all three names are accurate. Oh my, I've seen drawings but I've never seen an actual spanking chair."

Andrew runs his hand over the wide carved back, then stands in front of the chair with one hand on each arm exclaiming over the width of it. "Plenty of elbow-room here!" he declares with a chuckle. "And these slots built in to the side are meant to hold the spanking implements. Oh yes, paddles of different sizes and materials would fit nice and handy right here ready to be put to use. Too bad none of them survived over the years!"

Seating himself he tries to rock side to side but the chair doesn't budge. It's solid. "This is such a wide comfortable seat. Well, that makes sense..." he trails off, an image filling his mind's eye.

Lizzie gives him a quizzical look so he explains: "You would need to be comfortable if you're in for a lengthy session. After all, there could easily be half-a-dozen maids to be seen to. The design of this chair admirably serves its purpose."

"Yes, but what purpose is that?" Lizzie demands.

"Why, what it's named for, of course: spanking! The master of the house would sit in this chair and upend all the naughty females – servants and family alike – over his knee to administer their punishment.

I suppose in a very large wealthy household it might be the duty of the head butler but no, anyone who buys a purpose-built chair is going to enjoy doing the job himself.

I expect it would be a scheduled ritual, probably happening every Sunday - but after Church, they wouldn't want the girls painfully squirming in the pews!

Oh can you just imagine a line of girls, all anxiously crying, while they wait their turn? I'm sure the young ones covered their eyes and pretended not to watch but peeked through their fingers. Oh I wish I could draw! I'd love to capture the image that I've got in my mind right now.

I bet the lady of the house would be dealt with last to preserve her modesty while simultaneously drawing out the dreaded anticipation. How humiliating to have to bear witness knowing she'll soon be the one kicking up her heels," he concludes with a gleam of prurient satisfaction in his eye.

"Andrew, I know you're an historian but this is very esoteric... how do you know about it?"

"I mentioned I've seen drawings, yes? I can show you some later although I only have a small collection. You see they're quite expensive because there's a lot of interest in depictions of corporal punishment through the ages."

"Corporal... oh! But surely you aren't... oh!"

Giving her a wide smile Andrew replies: "Oh, indeed I am. The colloquialism is *spankophile* and let me tell you how I envy the original owner of this chair.

All those wiggling bottoms bared in invitation! Small, pretty, plump, in all shapes and sizes, completely at his mercy. What fun he must have had even if he had to disguise it as *good Christian discipline in a God-fearing household.*"

He titters a laugh saying: "The only thing those young women had to fear was the heavy hand of the Master of the House.

I wonder whose job it was to keep track of all the misdeeds that needed addressing? Or maybe each of the maids were spanked every week just as a matter of course, pre-emptive so to speak.

And Lizzie, now that I've sat in the chair it needs to be put to use, christened so to speak, you know, like drawing a sword from its scabbard, so come here."

Her eyes widen in surprise but her pupils dilate with lust. Fighting her rising blush she takes a deep breath but that only makes her hardened nipples more prominent. She refuses to acknowledge her traitorous body's reaction but Andrew doesn't miss a thing.

"No! I will not! Andrew, seriously, you can't possibly think I... I don't want—"

"Elizabeth!" his voice is stern. "Do not make me wait or it will be worse for you."

She gasps and shakes her head *no!* Andrew leaps up and grabbing hold of Lizzie's hand yanks her forward until he's back sitting in the chair and she's being maneuvered across his knee.

"You listen to me, Andrew Armitage," she hollers. "Let me go right now!"

"No, Elizabeth Parker. I'm not listening to you, I'm telling *you* to hear what *I* say. You're about to be soundly spanked, by my hand, on your bare bottom. It's my birthday and I'm going to enjoy celebrating it this way with you."

She screeches as he pushes up the skirt of her dress neatly tucking it under her right arm that he's got pinned to the small of her back. Andrew is right-handed so he's positioned Lizzie's torso to his left leaving plenty of room to swing his arm.

First, though, he teases her by scratching his fingertips across the satin of her panties. He muses aloud stating: "Many images show the miscreant fully nude for her punishment and I'm sure there's a valuable psychological aspect to that, but... I've always been enticed by the sight of a clothed body with only the derriere exposed – it seems to make the bottom appear even more naked, if that makes sense.

So these need to be taken down but only as far as mid-thigh." Studying the picture this makes he gives a contented sigh murmuring *perfect, just perfect."*

Lizzie is spluttering with indignation and can't form a clear, coherent sentence as she switches between angry *don't you dare* expostulations to pleading *Andrew, I beg you, please don't do this, it will change things between us.*

Every word is a stimulant to the strict enforcer lurking in Andrew's psyche. He's spent hours poring over his drawings and the pictures he's found in old reference books, searching out photos online, even watching live-action spankings on Internet porn sites, but he's never had this opportunity.

In a hoarse voice he admonishes Lizzie saying, "Elizabeth, you've been a very naughty girl who's earned herself a good old-fashioned spanking and I'm the man to deliver it. Uh-uh! Not another word or you'll get extra swats," he warns.

"You let me up right now Andrew or I'll—"

"That's an extra two, do you want to try for five?" Before the words are even out of his mouth he smacks her hard on each cheek. The white skin of her lovely heart-shaped bottom shows two pink handprints. Andrew sucks in his breath in appreciation and Lizzie utters two cries of *ouch, stop!* and *that hurts!*

"Right, that's an extra five. Elizabeth you're already getting seven strokes before your punishment has even begun! I was planning on spanking you to a nice pink color but if you keep this up you're going to be red-hot by time I'm done."

Lizzie keeps shouting out commands to *stop!* and each time Andrew delivers another firm swat. By time she finally has the sense to keep her mouth shut her plump globes are already rosy and quivering.

"Right! Now we can begin," Andrews gleefully declares while Lizzie wails in pain and protest, insisting her bottom already feels like it's on fire. Yet is hasn't escaped his notice that she's rubbing her mound against him, and the enticing glimpses he's getting of her pussy show that the tender flesh there is shiny with wetness.

Andrew determinedly begins spanking Lizzie with steady hard swats and decides that the smacking sounds mingled with her tearful cries are pure music.

"Your bottom is perfect, just perfect. Built for punishment and an exact fit for my hand. Although of course we'll explore other options... meaning other implements.

Not this time, though. No, for our first spanking my hand will do the job admirably. Oh Lizzie, seeing you squirming like this is exquisite. Thank you my dear for this wonderful gift."

Happily he remembers that Christmas isn't far off and being *hard-to-buy-for* means he can name his present and it will be Lizzie bare across his knee again!

Chuckling, he realizes this exceptional chair will have to be put to use much sooner because he can't possibly wait until December. In fact, he decides that at age 32 it's high time Lizzie was married so he'll propose – and soon.

I'll do it while cuddling her afterwards and tomorrow we'll go shopping for a ring, he decides.

That way he can institute a Sunday spanking routine in his own household, and the chair will be reinstated to its full glory.

The Fake Thief

En route to my lunch meeting I get a message canceling and end up returning to the office unexpectedly. Entering our anteroom I find my secretary raiding the petty cash box.

I don't know who is more shocked: me finding Mariel stuffing bills down her bra, or Mariel being caught in the act.

Not surprisingly I'm instantly angry. "Why are you stealing my money?" I thunder at her. "I manage your rich family's finances so I'm well aware that you have a huge monthly allowance. I don't even know why you bother to work."

Mariel is blushing furiously in shame at being caught, but also with arousal brought on by my stern tone. I recognize the signs. I've known since her first day here that she has a major crush on me.

In fact, I figure that's why she took this job that she doesn't need, doesn't enjoy, and isn't very good at.

Seeing her nipples have grown hard and hearing her shallow panting I realize she's turned on at being caught... at the threat of being punished. By me. I force myself to frown, otherwise I'll grin. I'm definitely up for some sexy fun with my pretty, young secretary.

"Go into my office, now!" I order and she scurries to obey.

Walking behind her my mind quickly calculates what I can do and the best way to proceed. Snibbing the lock in the door handle I stalk closer. It's thrilling to see how she cringes while at the same time licking her lips. Mixed messages, indeed.

"Take your clothes off."

Both the words and my matter-of-fact almost bored tone of voice startle her into squealing: *What?*

"You heard me. I have to check whether you've stolen and hidden anything else."

I slip out of my suit jacket and roll up my shirt sleeves before crossing my arms over my chest. She stares at my forearms then lets her gaze travel up over my biceps and across my well-developed chest. I work out every morning before starting my business day and I know she sees a strong man exuding a threatening presence.

Belatedly she protests: "I haven't taken anything else!"

"Yeah right, and I'm going to take your word for it? You're a thief Mariel, I don't believe a word you say. Now you'll have to prove to me you have nothing concealed so hurry up and get those clothes off."

Mariel stammers and blushes, curling into herself with a hunched back while slowly undressing. She dresses conservatively in office wear of a black skirt, white blouse, and hose. But the skirt hugs her curves, the blouse is made of a sheer silky material, and her stockings are tinged with the merest hint of black.

I stop her when she's stripped down to her white lacy camisole with matching thong, stay-up stockings and high-heels. Walking around her I pause several times to stare at the view for a long couple of minutes before ordering her to remove the camisole.

She beseeches me with tear-filled eyes but my face remains impassive. Casting her gaze down Mariel lifts the hem of the camisole and pulls it up over her head exposing her naked breasts. She immediately tries to cover them but I bark a command of *arms behind your back!*

She complies and that position pushes her tits forward so I take my time to study them. Although outwardly expressionless inside I'm admiring the perfection of their shape, the curved weight at the bottom, the darkening nipples tilted upwards. As I watch her skin goosebumps and the rosy buds tighten even more.

Pushing myself off the desk I've been leaning on I reach out to jostle the underside of her breasts with my fingertips pretending to check for contraband but really just to shame her.

Truth is I just wanted to touch that silky smoothness but when I see how she bows her head, trying to hide the way her face has colored up well... I leave her standing exposed while I toy with the perfect tits that are being offered for me to fondle. She stays perfectly still and keeps her hands behind her back.

When I tell she's being *a good girl* her whole body shudders at the praise and the sway of her pretty tits is mesmerizing.

Pushing myself off the desk I've been leaning on I instruct her to *bend over the desk and grip the far edge*. It's a stretch for her to reach and if she wasn't wearing heels her feet would be off the floor.

As it is her body of perfectly smooth, unmarked skin is beautifully laid out. With her arms over her head I can easily see how her breasts are squashed against the wood with a swell of side breast showing.

Her body undulates like a wave with her back dipping down at her waist and her hips lifting up an immensely spankable ass. The thong provides very little coverage but still I pull it down to the middle of her thighs.

"I need to check that nothing's been tucked in here," I say rubbing the fabric. "It feels wet... why is that, Mariel? Does being caught out as an incompetent thief excite you?" She groans with embarrassment and clenches her buttocks.

Capitalizing on her shame I continue: "Hmm, it's actually soaking wet. How mortifying to have this evidence of your arousal exposed to me. What do you like best, Mariel? Stripping naked for me? Lying down so obediently? Or anticipating what comes next?"

Maybe you'd like me to fondle your pretty bum, hmm?" I pinch a good chunk of her soft flesh then knead my hands all over her delectable rump. Her reaction shows me this is a powerful erogenous zone for her.

I pick up my mouse-pad, it's made of a smooth, supple leather, and remark that *this wrist-rest provides a good handle, I can grip it easily*. Then I place my left hand down on her bare back to hold her firmly in place.

"Should bad girls who steal money be punished Mariel?"

She sobs in reply but I demand a proper answer.

"Yes," she chokes out.

"Yes, what?"

With a gasp she answers: "Yes, sir!"

I sigh and continue: "Yes, sir what?"

Mariel gulps a deep breath before replying in a rush that *yes sir bad girls should be punished.*

"I agree. Now what is an appropriate punishment for a naughty girl?" This time I gently cup the plump mound of one buttock in my right hand. Once again I marvel at how her skin feels impossibly soft and the flesh is squishy. Eminently spankable!

"Would a sound spanking be appropriate? A sound spanking on the bad girl's bare bottom?"

Mariel remains silent because she's holding her breath.

"Answer me!" I demand in an angry tone of voice.

She tries to answer but struggles, stumbling over her words, before finally saying: "I don't know... maybe?"

"Maybe, what?"

"Maybe she should be punished with a sound spanking, sir," the words come out breathlessly.

"Hmm, yes. I think we're on the same page now. So we agree that the proper punishment for a naughty thief is a sound spanking on her bare bottom, correct?"

Crying now she whispers *yes, sir.*

"Come, come Mariel. You know I want you to answer in a full sentence. In fact, since we agree on this matter I'd like you to ask - no I'd like you to beg - me to punish you. To make everything right again. Go ahead."

"Oh! Oh sir, I can't!"

"You can and you will. Say it now unless you want to earn yourself some extra smacks, is that it?"

"No, no I don't want that. Please sir, please spank me soundly on my... my bare bottom."

"Why?"

The sound of her painfully indrawn breath is so stimulating.

"Because I deserve to be punished, sir."

"Why?" I repeat.

"Because I was stealing," her voice drops to a quiet mumble.

"Which makes you a...?"

"A thief, sir. I'm a thief."

"That's right. You're a self-confessed naughty thieving girl. Do you submit to your spanking willingly?"

She groans with the humiliation of this catechism before confirming that *yes, she is willing to be punished.*

She's so aroused her scent has wafted throughout my office and I'm getting lightheaded from inhaling so deeply. The power I hold right now is overwhelmingly erotic.

I'm convinced that if I hadn't returned early to catch her in the act Mariel would have left an obvious trail of clues leading right back to herself. She desperately wants to be dominated and disciplined by me. She craves it.

I start off strong and continue in a steady rhythm that soon has her pale flesh blooming a rosy pink before deepening to red. My delivery is even and measured for maximum impact on her very inviting derriere.

The mousepad is ideally suited and the loud snapping sound of leather cracking against bare skin almost drowns out her mewling cries. I'm placing each stroke precisely, taking my time to give maximum coverage. Then I change it up by striking the same spot repeatedly until she moans.

Unable to stay still Mariel writhes and shimmys futilely trying to evade the next smack. Although this spectacle is highly entertaining I remind her that she's asked for this punishment and to be still while it's administered.

She does her best and despite the involuntary flexes of her aching cheeks she meekly accepts her due until a few particularly stinging swats to her sit spot have her reaching back to cover herself .

My reprimand is harsh: "That's another six strokes added after I finish this spanking."

She pulls back her hands begging: "Oh no please sir, I'm sorry I couldn't help it."

Her pleas fall on deaf ears as I go on and on applying spank after spank. Mariel is kicking her legs and sobbing as each stroke burns her very red and obviously painful behind.

I think she looks positively edible. Especially since I can see the sheen of lubrication on her pink pussy lips as she wriggles enticingly. Every tantalizing glimpse shows me how turned on she is.

"That's enough for now," I state once she's sobbing and wilted in compliance. "I've decided I'll deliver the extra half-dozen tomorrow. I want you to spend the rest of the day today, and overnight while lying in your bed, thinking about what's in store for you.

I doubt that I'll stop at only six strokes. I expect your poor bottom will still be very sore but I won't hold back. I plan to give you a good walloping because that's the price you pay for thievery and disobedience."

"But tomorrow is Saturday," she reminds me.

"Excellent! We won't be disturbed and I can take my time. Now I want you to show up wearing a long dress with nothing on underneath. No bra, no panties. I want you to get ready in the morning and leave your house to travel in being very aware of your nudity, and how you are humbling yourself for me.

You will stay naked all day, you will follow my instructions without hesitation, you will be my compliant and obedient little slut, and you will submit to my very thorough correction without complaint. Then I'll know you have truly atoned for your crime. Do you understand and agree?"

"Oh yes, yes sir!"

"I can see that I've been too lax with you, young lady. I've let you get away with being a so-so employee who is sadly lacking in skills. You need to be taken in hand and trained properly.

So be forewarned that tomorrow you will get a lengthy punishment that includes corner time, orgasm denial, and begging. You'll experience a painful bottom along with exquisite and extreme humiliation. I'm looking forward to it. Now thank me, Mariel."

Tears are streaming down her face as she gasps: "Thank you sir."

I step back and gesture for her to get up. She's slightly off-balance and her breasts swing invitingly until she steadies herself. My hands ache to fondle, caress, and pinch those hard little points but this is punishment. I want her horny and embarrassed even if she does look positively edible.

I sit down behind my desk to watch her dress while hiding my own arousal. Mariel winces as she pulls her thong up over her sore behind and gets into the rest of her clothes quickly.

"Go wash your face in my bathroom and make yourself presentable before going back to your desk," I tell her.

She hurries to obey and when she's ready to leave I warn: "I'm going to enjoy watching you squirm in your chair for the rest of the afternoon. Make sure you check in with me at the end of your work day."

Mariel pauses at the door unaware that I had locked it. Her face is surprised until I tell her: "No one will ever see you naked except me, my naughty girl." She shivers as my words send a thrilling zing straight to her core.

For the rest of the afternoon Mariel suffers through the pain of her sore bum pressed into her ergonomic chair, and the shame of me noticing - and frequently chuckling - every time she squirms.

With great relief she rises when the clock shows five and knocking on the open door enters my office.

"Close the door and lock it," I order curtly. She does so, turning back to me with an apprehensive look as she worries her bottom lip. I decide to keep her in suspense to draw out her agitation.

I see that she can't help her eyes drifting to the expanse of desk where only a few short hours ago she was stretched out bare naked except for her lace-topped stockings awaiting her punishment. Women wear pretty lingerie for themselves, it make them feel sexy, and I can tell from the expression on her face that she's imagining how she looked lying there.

In her mind's eye she can picture her pale hair, pale skin, and sheer stockings contrasting dramatically with her reddened bottom quivering in anticipation of the next strike. The leather mousepad that smacked so harshly will now look innocuous.

"Tomorrow I'm going to put you across my knee for a hard hand-spanking and then I'll administer further correction with my belt." Her eyes widen in alarm and I give her a cruel smile.

"I do not give you permission to touch yourself between now and then. I expect your little pussy to have puffy swollen lips and a red needy clit. If it doesn't tomorrow's spanking will be far more severe than today's. Do you understand?"

"Yes, sir" she murmurs, her eyes now staring down at her feet.

"Look at me, Mariel."

Reluctantly she lifts her eyes to meet my undoubtedly cold gaze. "You do not need to steal money therefore when you do steal it's for attention and punishment. You want that from me and I'm going to give you plenty of both.

She murmurs a protest but I put my hand up to stop her saying: "Don't be a liar as well as a thief."

She swallows a sob and nods.

"Going forward I'm going to make you my little project. I will give your body all of my attention, particularly your delectable ass. I'm going to keep it in a state of rosy redness which means I'll need to inspect the color frequently throughout the day and maintain as required. I promise to give you the punishment you crave and... so desperately need."

Her cheeks flame scarlet with humiliation and I'm certain it's not just at the memory of me spanking her bare bottom with the leather pad, but with the awareness of how much she was turned her on then and now. I watch as her thighs move under the pencil skirt and know she's trying to squeeze her distended clit.

"This is all on you, Mariel. You have given yourself to me to be properly disciplined and I will use you however I see fit."

The long column of her slender throat pulses and I imagine those same swallows wrapping around my cock as I deep-throat her. Her punishments will give me endless pleasure. I notice that her nipples are hard again and poking the fabric of her blouse.

My smile is as cold as my eyes as I whisper in a low rumble: "I own you now and I will do whatever I want whenever I want. I will use your body in every possible way because you're mine."

She gives an involuntary jolt that quivers through her whole body.

"Now, give me your panties, your thong," I demand holding out my hand but she just stares at it. "Now, Mariel," I growl at her. "Take it off and give it to me."

Her eyes are bright with unshed tears as she obeys my order. Her skirt is so tight she has to pull it up high on her thigh to make room for her hands.

Hooking her fingers around the lacy band she tugs it down, flinching as it rubs against her well-spanked bottom, until finally she can slide the lacy scrap of material down her legs. With her shoes still on she carefully steps out of her lingerie and bending down scoops it up to deposit on my outstretched palm.

I chuckle and bring the damp thong to my nose and inhale deeply. Mortified by this, Mariel's tears spill down her cheeks. I give her a close-mouthed smirk as I pocket the panties. Before she can fix her skirt I hold out my hand again instructing her to *kiss the hand that punished so well* and *thank me for the correction.*

For a moment I wonder if I've pushed her too far. She simply stares at me with eyes and mouth forming round O shapes of surprise. After a couple of slow blinks she comes closer and bending down brushes her lips against my palm saying: "Thank you for punishing me, sir."

Before she can straighten up I say: "Uh-uh. Just saying the word *punishing* isn't good enough, is it Mariel? You know I want you to be far more... descriptive."

She briefly closes her eyes then mumbles: "Thank you for the spanking, sir."

"More!" I insist.

With a groan she adds to her thanks: "For the sound spanking on my... my... bare bottom, sir," she rushes out the last words in a gasp.

I had no idea I was a disciplinarian with a dominant streak until I had this lush girl's naked body at my mercy. Her pretty bottom tempted – no, invited - me to deliver a good old-fashioned spanking and many more will follow.

No wonder building my business always took priority over sex. Despite the large number of beautiful willing women I've bedded none has ever brought out this urge in me. It's got to be Mariel herself who encourages and entices this stern side of my personality.

"Turn around and show me if there's any color left on your backside," I instruct.

She turns away from me and with a wiggle finishes pulling the hem of her skirt right up. This exposure of just her naked rear, between the skirt at her waist and the stay-up stockings on her thighs, instantly makes me hard. Her plump cheeks are still rosy red. I get a great deal of satisfaction at seeing how well I marked her.

As Mariel starts to move I order: "Put your hands on top of your head and stay perfectly still." She does as she's told and I see her tremble while she holds the position.

Taking out my phone I snap a photo. Her head jerks when she hears the unmistakable click but she doesn't say a word. After keeping her standing like this for two solid minutes I tell her she may pull down her skirt and leave.

"Don't drive your car in tomorrow, Mariel. Take a cab or an Uber. I think I'll probably want to keep you overnight in order to give you the intensive punishment you've earned. Plus maximum embarrassment and shaming, of course. I want the blush on your face to rival the burning flame on your poor bottom. You're going to be a very sorry girl, begging to appease me."

She gasps, but her pupils are blown wide with arousal as she nods in agreement.

"And remember no touching allowed. I'll be giving your little pussy a close examination and will expect an instant orgasm with just my hot breath on your overstimulated clit."

Her shocked *Oh!* as she runs out the door makes me chuckle. I'm certainly going to enjoy teaching her a lesson, over and over again. And I'll definitely be giving my delightfully incompetent and slutty secretary a raise.

From the Author

Thank you for choosing *She's Getting It Again!* another book of short stories in the *She's Just Bad* series. I hope you enjoyed it!

A third collection of stories for this series is already begun.

Please consider leaving a rating or a review. These provide helpful information to other readers, and assist authors in rankings.

With appreciation,

Lucy

Also by Lucy Lafferty

She's Just Bad
She's Gonna Get It Now!
She's Getting It Again!

Standalone
Santa's Christmas Party with the Littles: a DD/lg Age Play and Age Gap
Short Story
A New Year's Resolution for Boss Daddy's Tardy Middle
A Valentine's Day Punishment for a Naughty Middle's Vandalism
Doll Learns a Different Lesson at the St Patrick's Day Masquerade
Dared to Bare
Easter Eggs For Sylvie
Tammy's April Fool's Prank
Celebrating the Fourth of July at Bandits BDSM Club
The Bandits BDSM Club Collection

Watch for more at https://lori-laidlaw-novelist-bvwonn.mailerpage.io/
projects-copy.

About the Author

Lucy writes teasing stories of dominant men giving their brats well-deserved OTK spankings. *Then the sexy fun begins!*

Read more at https://lori-laidlaw-novelist-bvwonn.mailerpage.io/projects-copy.

www.ingramcontent.com/pod-product-compliance
Lightning Source LLC
Chambersburg PA
CBHW020331130626
46549CB00003B/1122